EARTH'S NATURAL BIOMES

DESERT BIOMES

Louise and Richard Spilsbury

WAYLAND
www.waylandbooks.co.uk

First published in Great Britain in 2017 by Wayland

Editor: Hayley Fairhead
Design: Smart Design Studio
Map (page 7) by Stefan Chabluk

ISBN: 978 1 5263 0129 1
10 9 8 7 6 5 4 3 2 1

www.hachette.co.uk
www.hachettechildrens.co.uk

Printed and bound in China

All photographs except where mentioned supplied by
Nature Picture Library www.naturepl.com

Front cover(main) and p20(inset) Solvin Zanki; cover (tr), title page(main), p4 and p31(br) Steve O. Taylor (GHF); p5 Ann & Steve Toon; p6 and back cover(r) Rolf Nussbaumer; p7 Chris Mattison; p8, back cover(l) and title page(b) Rolf Nussbaumer; p9(main) Jack Dykinga, p10 and front cover(tl) Bruno D'Amicis; contents page(t) and p11(main) Stefan Widstrand; title page(t), p12(main) and p31(t) Solvin Zankl; imprint page(b) and p13 Ben Cranke; p14 Konstantin Mikhailov; p15 and p31(bl) Daniel Heuclin; p16 Fred Olivier; contents page(b) and p17 Visuals Unlimited; p18 Dave Watts; p19 and p32 Jose B. Ruiz; front cover(b) and p21(main) Marguerite Smits Van Oyen; p21 John Cancalosi; p22 Chadden Hunter; p23 Gavin Hellier; p25 Eric Baccega; imprint page(t) and P26 Daniel Heuclin; p27 Staffan Widstrand; p28 Roladn Seitre; p29 Ann & Steve Toon.

Photographs supplied by Shutterstock: p9(inset) Shihina; p11(inset) Laborant; p12(inset) EcoPrint; p24 Lukas Holub.

CONTENTS

WHAT IS A DESERT BIOME?

Most people think of deserts as hot and sandy, but there are several different kinds of desert. What makes a desert a desert is a lack of rain. Most deserts get less than 300 millimetres of rain a year, whereas 2,000 mm can fall in a rainforest every year.

Different deserts

Some deserts are large, flat expanses of sand, but others have rocks and mountains or hills of sand, called dunes, that can reach 400 metres high. Some deserts reach sizzling temperatures of 54 degrees Centigrade or more, while other deserts have chilly winters or are freezing cold all year, like Antarctica. Some deserts receive very light but regular rain showers, others get all their annual rain in one heavy storm that lasts for just an hour.

Only one in ten of the world's deserts has sand dunes. Most, like this one in northern Niger, are rocky with occasional plants.

Fact Focus: Biome or Habitat?

Biomes are regions of the world that have a similar climate, plants and animals, such as deserts, forests, rivers, oceans, tundra and grassland. A habitat is the specific place in a biome where a plant or animal lives.

Desert life

Some deserts look empty and lifeless. The lack of water and soil means that plants grow far apart, to get a share of any water available. But there is a rich variety of plant life, ranging from saguaro cactuses as tall as a four-storey house, to plants that look like tiny stones (see page 9). There are few trees to give shade, so although there are some large animals, such as camels, most desert-dwelling animals are small. Some, such as desert tortoises, have shells or tough, scaly skin to protect them from the fierce temperatures. Others, such as ground squirrels, make burrows under the ground to escape the daytime heat.

The Cape ground squirrel has a long, very bushy tail that it uses like a parasol to provide shade when it is feeding in the hot Kalahari Desert.

Amazing Adaptation

Adaptations are special features or body parts that living things develop over time to help them survive in a biome. Mammals, such as camels, that live in hot deserts have very furry backs to protect them from the burning sun.

WHERE ARE DESERTS?

Deserts cover about a fifth of the Earth's land surface and there are four different types: subtropical, coastal, rain shadow and polar.

Subtropical deserts

Many of the world's deserts, including the Sahara Desert in Africa and the Sonoran Desert in North America, are subtropical. Very hot, moist air rises above the Equator, condenses and falls as heavy tropical rains in rainforests. The air is now very dry as it moves to the north and south of the Equator, creating deserts in subtropical areas.

Polar deserts

Antarctica is the driest desert of all. More than 98 per cent of Antarctica is covered with ice and there is no rain, only snow, so there is almost no liquid water at all.

Amazing Adaptation

Couch's spadefoot toads shed layers of skin to create a watertight covering over its body. This stops water escaping so the toad can survive dry periods underground. These toads can eat enough insects in one or two nights to survive for up to a year.

The Sonoran Desert has two short rainy seasons, and then it's dry for months. To avoid the dry months, Couch's spadefoot toads stay underground for most of the year and only come out when it rains.

Coastal deserts

When air blows over a coast from a cold ocean, the water vapour in the air condenses to form fog. If the water droplets in this fog are too small to fall as rain and instead evaporate in the hot daytime sun, this creates coastal deserts, such as the Atacama Desert in Chile and the Namib Desert of South Africa.

Rain shadow deserts

Rain shadow deserts form where moist air is forced up one side of a mountain range. As the air rises it cools and condenses, falling as heavy rain. When the air travels down the other side of the mountain it is dry. The Gobi Desert in central Asia and Death Valley in the USA are rain shadow deserts.

Some deserts are caused by more than one factor. The Atacama is a coastal desert and suffers a rain shadow effect from the Andes Mountains.

Arctic Ocean

North America

Europe

Asia

Atlantic Ocean

Pacific Ocean

Africa

Pacific Ocean

South America

Indian Ocean

Australia

Coastal desert
Polar desert
Rain shadow desert
Subtropical desert

Antarctica

This map shows the location of the four different types of desert found around the world.

DESERT PLANTS

While there are different plants in hot deserts around the world, many have similar adaptations for surviving the heat and lack of water. Some desert plants can be seen all year, while others seem to magically reappear after heavy rains.

Collecting water

To collect water from droplets of fog or sudden rains, some desert plants, such as yuccas and agaves, have roots that spread far and wide just below the surface. Other plants, such as mesquite, have very long roots that reach water stores called aquifers deep underground. Many desert plants are succulents, plants that have thick fleshy stems, often with folds or grooves in them, which can swell to store water to use during the long dry periods.

Desert cacti provide food and shelter for a variety of desert animals. Tiny hummingbirds beat their wings quickly to hover at cactus flowers to sip their nectar.

Amazing Adaptation

Cactus plants are perfectly adapted for life in the desert. Cactus stems have folds that expand to store water after rains. Their leaves have become thin spines to minimise water loss.

Desert defences

Many desert plants have thorns or spikes to deter animals from eating them to get at their water supply. Living stone plants are succulents. Their leaves look like the stones among which they grow when they swell with stored water. This clever disguise hides the plants from animals that might try to eat them!

Instant flowers

Some desert plants, such as mallow, sand verbena and prickly poppies, often only appear after heavy rains. They grow when the ground is soaked and they produce flowers and seeds very quickly. The seeds sink underground and have a thick outer coat that allows them to survive there for a long time, ready to burst into life when it rains again.

Living stone plants look like tiny stones. You can only tell they are plants when they flower!

After heavy rains, some empty–looking deserts, such as this one in Arizona, USA, are suddenly covered with a carpet of brightly coloured flowers.

SUBTROPICAL DESERT LIFE

Animals that live in subtropical deserts face many challenges. Daytime temperatures are hotter than anywhere else on the planet, except inside volcanoes! And with few clouds to stop daytime warmth escaping, the nights are very cold.

Furry fox

In the Sahara Desert, the fennec fox digs large burrows to escape daytime heat and mostly hunts at night when it's cooler. Fennec foxes hunt animals, such as beetles and other insects, lizards and other reptiles, and get all the water they need from their food. Thick fur on the fox's back protects it from the blazing sun and keeps it warm at night. The sandy-coloured fur camouflages it in the desert and absorbs less heat than dark fur.

The fennec fox is small but its ears can be half the length of its body!

Amazing Adaptation

The fennec fox's big ears help it hear prey moving around in the dark and help to keep it cool. As warm blood passes through the many blood vessels in their large ears, heat escapes into the air.

Shifting sands

Many subtropical deserts are sandy or coarse and rocky. Sand is tricky to move across because it can shift and it can also get very hot. Fennec foxes have fur around their paw pads to protect their feet from hot sand and help them to grip the sand better. Camels have large, flat feet to spread their weight which stops them sinking into the sand. Sand fish lizards are named for the way they 'swim' just below the surface of the hot sand!

Amazing Adaptation

Camels have long eyelashes to keep out wind-blown sand. They can also close their nostrils, so they can walk through a sand storm unaffected!

Sand fish lizards have a long, narrow body, short legs and a pointed snout to help them move quickly beneath the sand.

COASTAL DESERT LIFE

Coastal deserts have cool winters to provide relief after the long, warm summers. Wildlife here can also access year-round moisture from early-morning sea fogs.

Trapping water

In the early morning, the Namib fog-basking beetle climbs to the top of a sand dune for a drink. It stands on its front legs with its body raised at an angle above its head. Fog blows in from the sea and water droplets in the fog stick to tiny bumps on its hard wings. Many droplets form drops that roll down waterproof grooves between the bumps and fall straight into the beetle's mouth!

The Namib fog-basking beetle, no bigger than a fingernail, collects its water supply from morning fog.

Amazing Adaptation

The weird Welwitschia plant of the Namib Desert has long, drooping leaves that grow flat across the land. Water droplets from morning fog condense on the leaves, which channel the droplets into the ground for the roots to soak up.

Desert chameleons

Most chameleons wait for prey to come to them, but those that live in deserts have to work harder as food is scarce. The Namaqua chameleon has toes that can spread to stop it sinking in Namib desert sand and help it run fast. It chases down and catches anything it can swallow, from beetles to snakes and scorpions, using its long tongue. This amazing animal has one other trick up its sleeve. In the morning, when it needs to warm up, it changes to a very dark colour to absorb the heat. In the hottest part of the day, it changes to a very light colour to keep cool.

The Namaqua chameleon's tongue is twice as long as its body, with a swollen sticky tip that shoots out to capture prey.

Fact File: Namib Desert

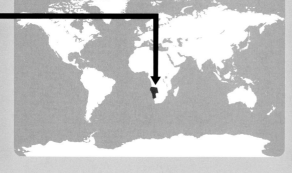

Location: West coast of southern Africa
Size: 81,000 square kilometres
Overview: The Namib Desert has vast gravel plains, scattered mountains and sand dunes that rise up to 300 m tall. Succulents grow near the coast but elsewhere there are very few plants.

RAIN SHADOW DESERT LIFE

Rain shadow deserts can be extreme places for animals to live. The Gobi Desert is very dry and has icy winters and burning hot summers. The Sonoran Desert is the hottest desert in North America.

Gobi gerbils

One animal that manages to survive in the Gobi Desert is the gerbil. Gerbils have sharp claws for digging underground burrows to escape danger and extremes of temperature. In summer they collect and store food, such as seeds, to survive the winter, when food is scarce. Groups of gerbils can stay underground for months when it is freezing. These tidy animals dig different burrows for storing food, sleeping and to use as a toilet!

The Mongolian gerbil's sand-coloured fur helps to camouflage it from predators. If a bird or snake grabs the gerbil by the tail, it loses its tail to escape and grows a new tail later!

Fact File: Gobi Desert

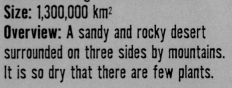

Location: Mongolia and China
Size: 1,300,000 km²
Overview: A sandy and rocky desert surrounded on three sides by mountains. It is so dry that there are few plants.

Rattlesnakes

Western diamondback rattlesnakes escape the Sonoran daytime heat in the shade of plants or rocks, or in underground burrows of other animals. In the winter, they hibernate in spaces in rocks to survive the cooler temperatures. Rattlesnakes also hunt for food in burrows. They have heat sensing pits behind each nostril that detect the heat given off by animals, such as mice and rats. This helps them to find their prey even in the total darkness underground. They bite into victims with their long fangs. These inject venom that stuns prey so the snake can swallow it down more easily.

A rattlesnake can shake the rattle at the end of its tail 60 or more times per second. Snakes grow by shedding old skin. Some rings of skin stay on the tail and harden to form rattles.

Amazing Adaptation

A rattlesnake's colours camouflage it in the desert, but if predators, such as eagles or other snakes, spot it, the rattlesnake hisses and rattles its tail to warn them off.

POLAR DESERT LIFE

The central desert region of Antarctica has so little water it is almost plant-free. It is colder here than anywhere else on Earth. Most of its wildlife is found at the coast, where the weather is milder.

Bird life

Some birds called petrels make nests on the bare rock on top of mountains that peek through the ice sheets. Giant petrels feed on penguins and other birds, and fish and squid from the ocean. Penguins have a thick layer of fat called blubber so they can survive on land and in the icy ocean, where they catch fish. Their short densely packed feathers help to keep out icy winds.

Male emperor penguins huddle together in the Antarctic desert to keep warm while they care for their chicks.

Amazing Adaptation

Most penguins build nests from piles of stones to protect their eggs from the cold. When a female emperor penguin lays an egg she passes it to the male. He balances it on his feet to keep it off the ice and nestles it among feathers that keep it warm.

Leopard seals

Leopard seals are found around the edges of the Antarctic continent. Like Antarctic penguins, leopard seals have a thick layer of blubber to insulate them from the cold. Leopard seals feed in the water and use their powerful jaws and long teeth to catch smaller seals, fish and squid. They haul themselves out onto ice sheets to rest. Females also have their pups on the ice sheets and dig small snow holes to keep their young safe while they grow.

Leopard seals are three to four metres long and are named because of their spotted fur. They move quickly and catch prey in water and on ice in their huge mouth full of sharp teeth.

Fact File: McMurdo Dry Valleys

Location: Antarctica, south of the Ross Sea
Size: 4,800 km²
Overview: The driest part of a huge, icy continent, found a few kilometres from the coast. There are giant slow-moving rivers of ice called glaciers and no rainfall, just a few centimetres of snow falls each year. The few living things in McMurdo include lichens, mosses and tiny animals, such as nematode worms.

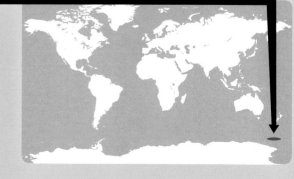

BORN SURVIVORS

Desert animals have some clever ways to make sure their young survive the extreme heat and the threat from predators.

Cactus crèche

A spiky cactus might not seem a very cosy place to bring up babies, but several desert birds build their nests in these plants because the spikes keep eggs and chicks safe from predators. For example, great horned owls build awkward-looking nests from sticks. Cactus wrens make football-shaped nests from grasses with an opening at one end. Gila woodpeckers lay about four white eggs in a nest inside a saguaro cactus!

The gila woodpecker's eggs and chicks are kept cool and safe from predators inside the cactus.

Amazing Adaptation

Gila woodpeckers have very strong head and neck muscles and a hard, long, pointed beak, which they use to peck holes in saguaro cactus, so they can make a nest inside.

Spider mums

Most spider mothers leave once they lay their eggs, but the tarantula is worse — she tries to eat her young! After she lays about 1,000 eggs in an underground burrow, the female tarantula seals it with a cover of silk. The eggs hatch after seven weeks and the young spiderlings cut holes in the silk cover and race away before their mother comes back to eat them!

Some desert spiders make excellent mothers, however. Female wolf spiders lay lots of eggs and wrap them in a bag of silk. They carry their eggs everywhere they go and search for them if they drop off. When the eggs hatch, the spiderlings climb up their mother's legs onto her back. They are safe from predators here. They stay on her back for several days until they are old enough to feed and defend themselves.

By keeping her eggs and then her hundreds of babies with her, the wolf spider can keep them at a comfortable temperature and protect them from predators.

DESERT FOOD CHAINS

A desert food chain tells the story of who eats who in the biome. Plants, such as cacti, use energy from the sun to make food. Some animals get the energy they need by eating the plants. But some animals feed on other animals as their energy source.

Energy in the Kalahari food chain flows from cacti and other plants, to eagles, via scorpions and meerkats.

Kalahari killers

Insects called termites build tall mounds of mud to shelter from the Kalahari Desert's heat and eat plants, such as dead cacti. Scorpions eat termites and meerkats enjoy a tasty scorpion or two! They quickly and carefully bite off the scorpion's stinger and spit it out so they can eat the animal. Meerkats take turns to look out for predators, while others feed. If the 'guards' spot an eagle they call out and all the meerkats run for safety in underground burrows.

Amazing Adaptation

The meerkat's long snout can sniff out scorpions and insects that hide in burrows by day. They use their curved claws to quickly dig holes in the sand to get their prey.

A scorpion can only get energy from prey, such as termites. It catches them first in its pincers and then stops them moving by using its stinger to jab deadly venom into them. Then the prey is easier to eat.

Cleaning up deserts

In deserts, as in other biomes, there is lots of natural waste to clear up, including the remains of animals that predators have killed and fed on, or which have died naturally, for example of old age. Scavengers are animals, such as vultures, coyotes and even worms, that feast on these scattered sources of dead meat.

The final links in the desert food chain are decomposers including bacteria. Decomposers eat fallen leaves, dead plants, animal poo and other waste including the remaining bits left over by scavengers. They gain energy as they feed but in the process also release nutrients into the desert soil that plants can use to grow and start new desert food chains.

Nothing is wasted in a desert: a turkey vulture scavenges the dried and rotting remains of a wild pig.

Fact Focus: Food Webs

Several food chains together form food webs. For example, desert termites are eaten by many animals from scorpions to toads, lizards and birds, and lizards may be eaten by many types of birds and snakes.

PEOPLE IN THE DESERT

The deserts of the world may lack water and suffer extreme temperatures, but they are still home to hundreds of millions of people!

Traditional lives

Some people who live in deserts grow crops on land around an oasis. An oasis is a place where water rises to the surface from an aquifer — a layer of underground rock which absorbs and holds water. Some farmers are nomads. They travel around and live in tents so they can move their flocks of goats, sheep, and camels to places where there are plants for the animals to eat, at the edge of deserts or where sudden rains fall.

Desert people often wear light-coloured robes because light colours reflect rather than absorb the sun's rays.

Amazing Adaptation

People have adapted to living in deserts by constructing buildings that keep them cool. Thick mud or clay walls insulate the interiors by absorbing heat. Tall wind towers capture breezes high above ground level and carry the cooler air deep inside. Any open spaces and windows are kept in the shade by overhanging roofs.

Growing cities

In spite of the lack of water, there are also huge cities in the middle of deserts, such as Dubai in the Arabian Desert and Las Vegas in the Mojave Desert. To get the water needed for drinking, washing, cooking and to grow large fields of crops for cities, people pump water up from deep aquifers. In some places they also divert rivers to water plants. Water from the Colorado River is piped to the desert in Imperial Valley, California to grow food.

Las Vegas is a huge city in the Mojave Desert, one of America's smallest and driest deserts.

Fact Focus: Water Problems

Desert aquifers are often filled with water that fell as rain a long way away and then gradually seeped there underground. When people take too much aquifer water for big farms or cities, desert plants that have deep roots and rely on aquifers for water cannot grow, leaving desert animals without food.

DESERT RESOURCES

Deserts may look empty, but beneath the rock, sand and gravel soils there are hidden treasures that people can use.

Finding fuels

Some deserts hold massive stores of oil and gas below their surface. Oil companies often have to drill hundreds of metres down to reach oil and gas supplies. Then pipelines carry the fuels for hundreds of kilometres across deserts to users or to ports, from where giant ships called tankers deliver it to buyers.

This is an oil well in the United Arab Emirates. Millions of years ago, the region was covered in ocean water. Animals that died in these ancient seas gradually formed fossil fuels.

Fact Focus: Antarctic Resources

So far, the Antarctic desert's resources are untapped because no one country owns Antarctica. Nations of the world have signed an Antarctic Treaty that allows them to carry out scientific research there, but not to do any drilling for oil or minerals. One reason is that transporting oil from here by ship would be risky and oil spills could ruin this wild habitat.

Mining minerals

There are also useful and valuable minerals, such as gold and copper beneath deserts. Gold is used to make gold bars or jewellery. Copper is a red metal that electricity can flow through so it is used to make electrical wire and parts of electrical equipment. People dig mines to reach desert minerals like these. The problem is that miners may use substances to extract minerals from rocks that can pollute desert aquifers. They also use water to clean minerals. This reduces the amount of water available for plants.

These men are digging up slabs of salt from the desert in Ethiopia.

Fact Focus: Salt Mines

In some places people dig for salt, too. The salt is found in desert regions where there were seas millions of years ago, when the areas were cooler. As the water evaporated, salt was left behind.

DESERT THREATS

The desert is an important and useful biome, but people are at risk of damaging it and destroying parts of it forever.

Global warming

At the same time as people are taking more water from deserts for cities and farms, global warming is making deserts drier too. Global warming is the gradual increase in the Earth's temperature. Rising temperatures cause droughts, when no rain falls, and mean more water evaporates into the air, making dry desert soils even drier and making oases dry up.

Dorcas gazelles in the Sahara Desert can get all the water they need from plants they eat. However, drought and overgrazing reduce the plant life and put these beautiful animals at risk.

Fact Focus: Animals Under Threat

Droughts reduce the plant life that grows in deserts and when it is hotter animals spend more time in burrows. This means there is less food for desert animals to eat and they have less time to find it.

Overgrazing

Overgrazing is when farmers allow too many cattle, goats, or sheep to feed on an area of land where there are few plants. The farm animals eat all the plants, and their hooves damage the newly bare soil, making it even drier and dustier and harder for new plants to grow there. This leaves fewer plants for wild desert animals to eat in the future.

Habitat destruction

People take over desert habitats when they build towns, roads and mines. Rare animals, such as grey kangaroos, risk being run over when crossing desert roads. But when tourists visit deserts, they often travel in off-road vehicles. These can crush plants and their delicate root networks, making it harder for them to grow. Vehicles can also collapse underground burrows where animals, such as desert tortoises and toads, spend much of their time.

Off-road vehicles damage desert soils and sand, so they blow or wash away more easily, and are noisy enough to disturb shy desert animals, including kangaroo rats.

DESERT FUTURES

Around the world, many people are working hard to protect fragile desert biomes and the living things adapted to their inhospitable environments, to ensure their survival for the future.

Scientific study

Scientists study desert biomes to work out what the problems are and what causes them. For example, they measure animals, such as desert tortoises, to see if changes in a desert affect their growth. They fit animals with radio collars that can track their movements to see how far they have to go to find food.

Solar Power

Some scientists are looking at ways to build huge solar power plants in deserts that use the uninterrupted sunlight there to make electricity. This would reduce the amount of oil and coal used to make electricity and reduce the impacts of global warming.

These scientists are studying the endangered African spurred tortoise in the Sahel Desert, West Africa.

Brown hyenas are desert animals under threat, but many live safely in the Kgalagadi Transfrontier National Park.

Conservation counts

Conservation groups work to conserve or protect wild places. Some work with governments to create national parks. These are areas of protected land where people cannot build, dig mines or take too much water. Conservation groups also raise money to help protect endangered desert animals.

We can all help desert biomes by supporting conservation organisations. We can also help by reducing our use of fossil fuels to slow global warming, for example by car-sharing or walking to school rather than going by car. What can you do to help?

Fact File: Kgalagadi Transfrontier Park

Location: Botswana and South Africa
Size: 37,000 km²
Overview: A huge park with dry landscapes and red sand dunes and animals, such as jackals, brown hyenas and wild cats.

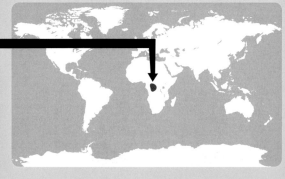

GLOSSARY

adaptation special feature or way of behaving that helps a living thing survive in its habitat.

algae plant-like living things that grow in damp places.

aquifer an underground layer of rock or soil that has holes that store water.

biome large region of Earth with living things adapted to the typical climate, soils and other features.

blood vessels tubes inside an animal that carry blood around its body.

blubber thick layer of fat under the skin

camouflage colour, pattern or shape that makes it hard to identify an object against the background it is in.

climate typical weather pattern through the year in an area

condense to change from a gas into a liquid.

conservation the act of guarding, protecting or preserving something.

continent one of the seven large masses of land on the planet: Asia, Africa, North America, South America, Europe, Australia and Antarctica

drought when an area gets so little water or rain that plants die.

dune hills formed from sand

endangered at risk of dying out

energy the power to grow, move and do things.

Equator imaginary line around the centre of the Earth

evaporate turn from a liquid into a gas.

food chain way of showing animals that eat each other as links in a chain.

food web feeding relationships between living things

global warming rise in average temperature of Earth caused by human use of machines and electricity, which is altering weather patterns worldwide.

habitat place where an animal or plant lives.

hibernate to go into a special type of deep sleep when body processes slow down to reduce use of stored food in an animal over winter.

insect animal such as a fly or beetle that has six legs and usually one or two pairs of wings.

insulate to prevent the movement of heat

lichen lifeform that is a partnership between two types of living things, fungi and algae.

mammal group of animals that have hair or fur and feed their babies with milk from their bodies.

mineral a substance such as salt that is non-living and forms naturally in or under the ground.

national park an area in nature where the wildlife is protected by law.

nectar sugary substance found in the centre of flowers.

nomad people who move from place rather than settling in one place.

oasis area in a desert where there is water and plants.

pits dips or indentations

pollute to allow substances, such as oil or smoke, to damage water, soil or the air.

predator animal that catches and eats other animals.

prey animal eaten by another animal.

reflect bounce off.

reptile a snake, lizard or other animal has cold blood, lays eggs, and has a body covered with scales or hard parts.

resources things that people use or need, like water and food.

solar power electricity made from sunlight.

South Pole southernmost point of the Earth

succulent plant with thick fleshy leaves or stems adapted to storing water.

venom poison made by some animals for defence or to stun or kill prey.

water vapour a gas in the air, formed when liquid water evaporates.

FIND OUT MORE

Books
Habitats (Science Skills Sorted!)
Anna Claybourne
Franklin Watts, 2017

Discover Science: Deserts
Dr. Nicola Davies
Kingfisher, 2017

**Grassland Food Webs in Action
(Searchlight Books: What Is a Food Web?)**
Paul Fleisher
Lerner Classroom, 2015

Desert Climates (Heinemann Infosearch: Focus on Climate Zones)
Anita Ganeri
Scholastic, 2016

Websites
Read more about deserts at:

kids.nceas.ucsb.edu/biomes/desert.html

There is more information about deserts at:

www.cotf.edu/ete/modules/msese/earthsysflr/desert.html

Explore the Sahara Desert at:

www.pbs.org/sahara/wildlife

Discover more about deserts at:

**environment.nationalgeographic.com/environment/
habitats/desert-profile/**

INDEX